Dear Parent:

Congratulations! Your child is taking
the first steps on an exciting journey.
The destination? Independent reading!

STEP INTO READING® will help your child get there. The program offers
five steps to reading success. Each step includes fun stories and colorful art.
There are also Step into Reading Sticker Books, Step into Reading Math
Readers, Step into Reading Write-In Readers, Step into Reading Phonics
Readers, and Step into Reading Phonics First Steps! Boxed Sets—a complete
literacy program with something for every child.

Learning to Read, Step by Step!

Ready to Read **Preschool–Kindergarten**
• big type and easy words • rhyme and rhythm • picture clues
For children who know the alphabet and are eager to
begin reading.

Reading with Help **Preschool–Grade 1**
• basic vocabulary • short sentences • simple stories
For children who recognize familiar words and sound out
new words with help.

Reading on Your Own **Grades 1–3**
• engaging characters • easy-to-follow plots • popular topics
For children who are ready to read on their own.

Reading Paragraphs **Grades 2–3**
• challenging vocabulary • short paragraphs • exciting stories
For newly independent readers who read simple sentences
with confidence.

Ready for Chapters **Grades 2–4**
• chapters • longer paragraphs • full-color art
For children who want to take the plunge into chapter books
but still like colorful pictures.

STEP INTO READING® is designed to give every child a successful
reading experience. The grade levels are only guides. Children can progress
through the steps at their own speed, developing confidence in their
reading, no matter what their grade.

Remember, a lifetime love of reading starts with a single step!

These are the Spanish words in this book:

abuela: ah-BWAY-lah
means "grandmother"

delicioso: deh-lee-see-OH-so
means "delicious"

sí: SEE
means "yes"

For Mary Evalyn Biggs Jones—J.H.
For Lizet, Evelyn, and Joscelyne—S.G.

Text copyright © 2003 by Judith Head. Illustrations copyright © 2003 by Susan Guevara. All rights reserved under International and Pan-American Copyright Conventions. Published in the United States by Random House Children's Books, a division of Random House, Inc., New York, and simultaneously in Canada by Random House of Canada Limited, Toronto.

www.stepintoreading.com

Educators and librarians, for a variety of teaching tools, visit us at
www.randomhouse.com/teachers

Library of Congress Cataloging-in-Publication Data
Head, Judith, 1944–
Mud soup / by Judith Head ; illustrated by Susan Guevara. p. cm. — (Step into reading. A step 3 book)
SUMMARY: Josh tries to avoid eating the "mud soup" prepared by Rosa's *abuela* (grandmother). Includes a recipe for black bean soup.
ISBN 0-375-81087-0 (trade) –– ISBN 0-375-91087-5 (lib. bdg.)
[1. Soups—Fiction. 2. Mexican Americans—Fiction.] I. Guevara, Susan, ill. II. Title. III. Step into reading.
Step 3 book. PZ7.H34225 Mu 2003 [Fic]—dc21 00-068410

Printed in the United States of America First Edition 10 9 8 7

STEP INTO READING, RANDOM HOUSE, and the Random House colophon are registered trademarks of Random House, Inc.

Mud Soup

by Judith Head

illustrated by
Susan Guevara

Random House 🏠 New York

Rosa smacked her lips.
She dipped her spoon
into her cup.

She slurped her soup.

"Mmm. Mud soup," she said.

"Delicioso."

Josh stared at his sandwich.
Clumps of peanut butter
hung from the edges.
Purple jelly oozed
through the bread.

"That looks lousy," Rosa said.

She handed Josh her thermos.

"Have some mud soup," she said.

Josh's stomach jumped.

His heart thumped.

The soup inside the thermos

was thick and dark.

He could see something

wiggling on the top

of the soup.

It looked a little like a bean.

But it looked a little

like a worm, too.

Josh held the soup

far away from him.

He tried not to look.

He did not want to eat a worm.

But he did not want

to hurt Rosa's feelings, either.

He handed the thermos

back to her.

"I like peanut butter

and jelly better," he said.

At noon on Saturday,

Josh rode his bicycle in the park.

He stopped next to the slide.

"I'm hungry," he said.

Rosa zipped down the slide.

"Me too," she said.

"Let's eat lunch at my house.

It's closer."

"Okay," Josh said.

Josh and Rosa went

to Rosa's house.

They walked into Rosa's kitchen.

A big pot stood on the table.

Steam circled out of it.

Rosa smacked her lips.

"Mmm. Mud soup," she said.

"*Delicioso.*"

Josh's stomach jumped.

His heart thumped.

He could see something

floating on the top

of the soup.

It looked a little like a bean.

But it looked a little

like a clump of dirt, too.

Josh did not want to eat dirt.

But he did not want

to hurt Rosa's feelings, either.

"I'm not hungry after all,"

he said.

He rushed out the door.

After school one day,

Josh rode his bicycle

to Rosa's house.

Rosa was riding her bike

on the sidewalk.

Her mama and *abuela*

were working in the garden.

Rosa's mama picked
onions and peppers.
She laid them in a basket.
Rosa's *abuela*
scooped mud into a pail.

A glob of mud slid down
the side of the pail.
A large ant crawled
on top of the pail.

"Would you like to stay

for dinner, Josh?"

Rosa's *abuela* asked.

"We are having soup," she said.

"*Sí*," said Rosa. "Mud soup."

Josh's stomach jumped.

His heart thumped.

He looked at the glob of mud

that ran down

the side of the pail.

He watched the ant

crawl across

the top of the pail.

He did not want to eat mud.

He did not want to eat an ant.

But he did not want
to hurt anyone's feelings, either.

"No thanks," he said.

He rode to the park
as fast as he could.

On International Day at school,
some of the parents
brought lunch.

Bobby's father brought

Chinese wontons.

Helen's father brought

little Greek cakes

dripping with honey.

Rosa's mama
stood beside a large pot.
Steam circled out of it.
She filled two bowls.
She handed one to Josh
and one to Rosa.
"Mmm. Mud soup," Rosa said.
"Delicioso."

Josh's stomach jumped.

His heart thumped.

The soup was thick and dark.

He could see something

swimming on the top

of the soup.

It looked a little like a bean.

But it looked a little

like a beetle, too.

Josh's face felt hot and sweaty.

His eyes grew big.

"I don't want to eat mud," he said.

Rosa smiled.

"There is no mud
in mud soup," she said.
"My *abuela* from Mexico
makes it with black beans."

Josh looked at the soup.
"Then why do you call it
mud soup?" he asked.

Rosa swallowed
a spoonful of soup.
"Because it looks a little like mud,"
she said.

Josh dipped his spoon into
the thick, dark soup.
He tasted it.

"Mmm," he said. "Yummy.
Mud soup is *delicioso*!"

Mud Soup

Get a grown-up to help you!

- 2 cups of dry black beans
- 3 tablespoons of olive oil
- 1 small onion, chopped
- 1 bay leaf
- salt

Wash the beans. Put them in a pot with 6 cups of water. Soak them for 4–8 hours. Drain them and put them back into the pot. Add 6 cups of water. Add the oil, the onion, and the bay leaf. Simmer for 1–2 hours, until the beans are tender. (Be sure they are always covered with water.) Add salt and stir.

Mmm. Yummy! *Delicioso!*